The Original Adventures of
RAGGEDY ANDY

❖—❖—❖—❖—❖

The Original Adventures of
RAGGEDY ANDY

❖ *Johnny Gruelle* ❖

DERRYDALE BOOKS
New York

This 1988 edition is published by Derrydale Books, distributed by Crown Publishers, Inc., 225 Park Avenue South, New York, New York 10003, by arrangement with Macmillan, Inc.

RAGGEDY ANN and RAGGEDY ANDY and all related characters appearing in this book are trademarks of Macmillan, Inc.

Manufactured in Italy

Library of Congress Cataloging-in-Publication Data

Gruelle, Johnny, 1880?–1938.
 The original adventures of Raggedy Andy.

 Previously published as: Raggedy Andy stories.
 Summary: Adventures of the doll Raggedy Andy,
including ''The Rabbit Chase,'' ''The New Tin Gutter,''
and ''Doctor Raggedy Andy''
 [1. Dolls—Fiction] I. Title.
PZ7.G9324Rag 1988b   [E]   88-3704
ISBN 0-517-66582-4

h g f e d c b a

To
Marcella's Mama

Gainesville, Florida

Johnny Gruelle
South Norwalk
Connecticut

Dear Johnny:

WHEN I saw your *Raggedy Ann* books and dolls in a store near here, I went right in and bought one of each, and when I had read your introduction to *Raggedy Ann* I went right up to an old trunk in my own attic and brought down the doll I am sending you with this letter.

This doll belonged to my mother and she played with it when a little girl. She treasured it highly, I know, for she kept it until I came and then she gave it to me.

The fun that we two have had together I cannot begin to tell you, but often, like the little boy who went out into the garden to eat worms when all the world seemed blue and clouded, this doll and I went out under the arbor and had our little cry together. I can still feel its soft rag arms (as I used to imagine) about me, and hear the words of comfort (also imaginary) that were whispered in my ear.

As you say in your *Raggedy Ann* book, "Fairyland must be filled with rag dolls, soft loppy rag dolls who go through all the beautiful adventures found there, nestling in the crook of a dimpled arm." I truly believe there is such a Fairyland and that rag dolls were first made there, or how

else could they bring so much sunshine into a child's life?

All the little girls of my acquaintance have your *Raggedy Ann* book and doll, and for the happiness you have brought to them, let me give to you the doll of all my dolls, the doll I love most dearly.

May it prove to you a gift from Fairyland, bringing with it all the "wish come true" that you may wish and, if possible, add to the sunshine in your life.

My mother called the doll Raggedy Andy and it was by this name that I have always known him. Is it any wonder that I was surprised when I saw the title of your book?

Introduce Raggedy Andy to Raggedy Ann, dear Johnny. Let him share in the happiness of your household.

Sincerely yours,

Raggedy Andy's "Mama"

Dear John:

YOUR LETTER brings many pleasant memories to my mind and takes me back to my childhood.

Living next door to us, when I was about four years old, was a little girl named Bessie. I cannot recall her last name. When my mother made Raggedy Ann for me, Bessie's mother made a rag doll for her, for we two always played together. As I recall, there was no fence between our two houses.

Bessie's doll was made a day or so after Raggedy Ann, I think, though I am not quite certain which of the dolls was made first. However, Bessie's doll was given the name of Raggedy Andy, and one of the two dolls was named after the other, so that their names would sound alike.

We children played with the two rag dolls most of the time until Bessie's family moved away—when I was eight or nine years old. They had faces just alike. The mother who made the first doll probably painted both doll faces. I do not remember just how Raggedy Andy was dressed, but I know he often wore dresses over his boy clothes when Bessie and I decided that he and Raggedy Ann should be sisters for the day.

You remember I told you about Raggedy Andy long ago. Isn't it strange that the two old rag dolls should come together after all these years? I wish Raggedy Andy's "Mama" had signed her name, for I should like to write to her. Perhaps there may be some way of finding her out.

Anyway, it seems to me you have the subject for another rag doll book, for Raggedy Andy must have had some wonderful adventures in his long life.

Yours lovingly,

Mom

HOW RAGGEDY ANDY CAME

ONE DAY Daddy took Raggedy Ann down to his office and propped her up against some books upon his desk. He wanted to have her where he could see her cheery smile all day, for, as you must surely know, smiles and happiness are truly catching.

Daddy wished to catch a whole lot of Raggedy Ann's cheeriness and happiness and put all this down on paper, so that those who did not have Raggedy Ann dolls might see just how happy and smiling a rag doll can be.

So Raggedy Ann stayed at Daddy's studio for three or four days.

She was missed very, very much at home and Marcella really longed for her, but knew that Daddy was borrowing some of Raggedy Ann's sunshine, so she did not complain.

Raggedy Ann did not complain either, for in addition to the sunny, happy smile she always wore (it was painted on), Raggedy Ann had a candy heart, and of course no one (not even a rag doll) ever complains if they have such happiness about them.

One evening, just as Daddy was finishing his day's work, a messenger boy came with a package—a nice, soft lumpy package.

Daddy opened the nice, soft lumpy package and found a letter.

1

Grandma had told Daddy, long before this, that at the time Raggedy Ann was made, a neighbor lady had made a boy-doll, Raggedy Andy, for her little girl, who always played with Grandma.

And when Grandma told Daddy this she wondered whatever had become of her little playmate and the boy-doll, Raggedy Andy.

After reading the letter, Daddy opened the other package which had been inside the nice, soft, lumpy package and found —Raggedy Andy!

Raggedy Andy had been carefully folded up. His soft, loppy arms were folded up in front of him and his soft, loppy legs were folded over his soft, loppy arms, and they were held this way by a rubber band.

Raggedy Andy must have wondered why he was being arranged this way, but it could not have caused him any worry, for in between where his feet came over his face Daddy saw his cheery smile.

After slipping off the rubber band, Daddy smoothed out the wrinkles in Raggedy Andy's arms and legs.

Then Daddy propped Raggedy Ann and Raggedy Andy up against books on his desk, so that they sat facing each other. Raggedy Ann's shoe-button eyes looking straight into the shoe-button eyes of Raggedy Andy.

They could not speak—not right out before a real person—so they just sat there and smiled at each other.

Daddy could not help reaching out his hands and feeling their throats.

Yes! There was a lump in Raggedy Ann's throat, and there was a lump in Raggedy Andy's throat. A cotton lump, to be sure, but a lump nevertheless.

"So, Raggedy Ann and Raggedy Andy, that is why you cannot talk, is it?" said Daddy.

"I will go away and let you have your visit to yourselves, although it is good to sit and share your happiness by watching you."

Daddy then took the rubber band and placed it around Raggedy Ann's right hand and around Raggedy Andy's right hand, so that when he had it fixed properly they sat and held each other's hands.

Daddy knew they would wish to tell each other all the wonderful things that had happened to them since they had parted more than sixty years before.

So, locking his studio door, Daddy left the two old rag dolls looking into each other's eyes.

Then next morning, when Daddy unlocked his door and looked at his desk, he saw that Raggedy Andy had fallen over so that he lay with his head in the bend of Raggedy Ann's arm.

THE NURSERY DANCE

WHEN Raggedy Andy was first brought to the nursery he was very quiet.

Raggedy Andy did not speak all day, but he smiled pleasantly to all the other dolls. There was Raggedy Ann, the French doll, the little Dutch doll, the tin soldier, Uncle Clem and a few others.

Some of the dolls were without arms and legs.

One had a cracked head. She was a nice doll, though, and the others all liked her very much.

All of them had cried the night Susan (that was her name) fell off the toy box and cracked her china head.

Raggedy Andy did not speak all day.

But there was really nothing strange about this fact, after all.

None of the other dolls spoke all day, either.

Marcella had played in the nursery all day and of course they did not speak in front of her.

Marcella thought they did, though, and often had them saying things which they really were not even thinking of.

For instance, when Marcella served water with sugar in it and little oyster crackers for "tea," Raggedy Andy was thinking of Raggedy Ann, and the French doll was thinking of one time when Fido was lost.

Marcella took the French doll's hand and passed a cup of tea to Raggedy Andy, and said, "Mr. Raggedy Andy, will you have another cup of tea?" as if the French doll was talking.

And then Marcella answered for Raggedy Andy, "Oh, yes, thank you! It is so delicious!"

Neither the French doll nor Raggedy Andy knew what was going on, for they were thinking real hard to themselves.

Nor did they drink the tea when it was poured for them. Marcella drank it instead.

Perhaps this was just as well, for most of the dolls were moist inside from the tea of the day before.

Marcella did not always drink all of the tea. Often she poured a little down their mouths.

Sugar and water, if taken in small quantities, would not give the dolls colic, Marcella would tell them, but she did not know that it made their cotton or sawdust insides quite sticky.

Quite often, too, Marcella forgot to wash their faces after a ''tea,'' and Fido would do it for them when he came into the nursery and found the dolls with sweets upon their faces.

Really, Fido was quite a help in this way, but he often missed the corners of their eyes and the backs of their necks, where the tea would run and get sticky. But he did his best and saved his little mistress a lot of work.

No, Raggedy Andy did not speak. He merely thought a great deal.

One can, you know, when one has been a rag doll as long as Raggedy Andy had. Years and years and years and years!

Even Raggedy Ann, with all her wisdom, did not really know how long Raggedy Andy and she had been rag dolls.

If Raggedy Ann had a pencil in her rag hand and Marcella guided it for her, Raggedy Ann could count up to ten —sometimes. But why should one worry one's rag head about one's age when all one's life has been one happy experience after another, with each day filled with love and sunshine?

Raggedy Andy did not know his age, but he remembered many things that had happened years and years and years ago, when he and Raggedy Ann were quite young.

It was of these pleasant times Raggedy Andy was think-

ing all day, and this was the reason he did not notice that Marcella was speaking for him.

Raggedy Andy could patiently wait until Marcella put all the dollies to bed and left them for the night, alone in the nursery.

The day might have passed very slowly had it not been for the happy memories that filled Raggedy Andy's cotton-stuffed head.

But he did not even fidget.

Of course, he fell out of his chair once, and his shoe-button eyes went *"Click!"* against the floor, but it wasn't his fault. Raggedy Andy was so loppy he could hardly be placed in a chair so that he would stay, and Marcella jiggled the table.

Marcella cried for Raggedy Andy, *"AWAA! AWAA!"* and picked him up and snuggled him and scolded Uncle Clem for jiggling the table.

Through all this Raggedy Andy kept right on thinking his pleasant thoughts, and really did not know he had fallen from the chair.

So you see how easy it is to pass over the little bumps of life if we are happy inside.

And Raggedy Andy was quiet all day, and the day finally passed.

Raggedy Andy was given one of Uncle Clem's clean white nighties and shared Uncle Clem's bed. Marcella kissed them all good night and left them to sleep until morning.

But as soon as she left the room all the dolls sat up in their beds. When their little mistress' footsteps passed out of hearing, all the dollies jumped out of their beds and gathered around Raggedy Andy.

Raggedy Ann introduced them one by one and Raggedy Andy shook hands with each.

"I am very happy to know you all," he said in a voice

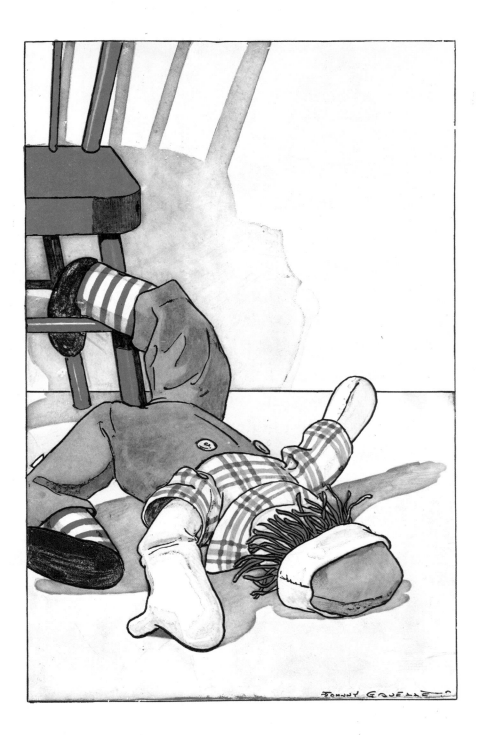

9

as kindly as Raggedy Ann's, "and I hope we will all like each other as much as Raggedy Ann and I have always liked each other!"

"Oh, indeed we shall!" the dollies all answered. "We love Raggedy Ann because she is so kindly and happy, and we know we shall like you, too, for you talk like Raggedy Ann and have the same cheery smile!"

"Now that we know each other so well, what do you say to a game, Uncle Clem?" Raggedy Andy cried, as he caught Uncle Clem and danced about the floor.

The Dutch doll dragged the little square music box out into the center of the room and wound it up. Then all,

holding hands, danced in a circle around it, laughing and shouting in their tiny doll voices.

"That was lots of fun!" Raggedy Andy said, when the music stopped and all the dolls had taken seats upon the floor facing him. "You know, I have been shut in a trunk up in an attic for years and years and years."

"Wasn't it very lonesome in the trunk all that time?" Susan asked in her queer little cracked voice.

"Oh, not at all," Raggedy Andy replied, "for there was always a nest of mice down in the corner of the trunk. Cute little Mama and Daddy mice, and lots of little teeny-weeny baby mice. And when Mama and Daddy mice were away, I used to cuddle the tiny little baby mice!"

"No wonder you were never lonesome!" said Uncle Clem, who was very kind and loved everybody and everything.

"No, I was never lonesome in the old trunk in the attic, but it is far more pleasant to be out again and living here with all you nice friends!" said Raggedy Andy.

And all the dolls thought so, too, for already they loved Raggedy Andy's happy smile and knew he would prove to be as kindly and lovable as Raggedy Ann.

THE RABBIT CHASE

"WELL, what shall we play tonight?" asked the Dutch doll when the house was quiet and the dolls all knew that no one else was awake.

Raggedy Andy was just about to suggest a good game, when Fido, who sometimes slept in a basket in the nursery, growled.

All the dollies looked in his direction.

Fido was standing up with his ears sticking as straight in the air as loppy puppy-dog ears can stick up.

"He must have been dreaming!" said Raggedy Andy.

"No, I wasn't dreaming!" Fido answered. "I heard something go, *'Scratch! Scratch!'* as plain as I hear you!"

"Where did the sound come from, Fido?" Raggedy Andy asked when he saw that Fido really was wide awake.

"From outside somewhere!" Fido answered. "And if I could get out without disturbing all the folks, I'd run out and see what it might be! Perhaps I had better bark!"

"Please do not bark!" Raggedy Andy cried as he put his rag arm around Fido's nose. "You will wake up everybody in the house. We can open a door or a window for you and let you out, if you must go!"

"I wish you would. Listen! There it is again— *'Scratch! Scratch!'* What can it be?"

"You may soon see!" said Raggedy Andy. "We'll let you out, but please don't sit at the door and bark and bark to get back in again, as you usually do, for we are going to play a good game and we may not hear you!"

"You can sleep out in the shed after you have found out what it is," said Raggedy Andy.

As soon as the dolls opened the door for Fido, he went running across the lawn, barking in a loud shrill voice. He

13

ran down behind the shed and through the garden, and then back toward the house again.

Raggedy Andy and Uncle Clem stood looking out of the door, the rest of the dolls peeping over their shoulders, so when something came jumping through the door, it hit Uncle Clem and Raggedy Andy and sent them flying against the other dolls behind them.

All the dolls went down in a wiggling heap on the floor.

It was surprising that the noise and confusion did not wake Daddy and the rest of the folks, for just as the dolls were untangling themselves from each other and getting up on their feet, Fido came jumping through the door and sent the dolls tumbling again.

Fido quit barking when he came through the door.

''Which way did he go?'' he asked, when he could get his breath.

''What was it?'' Raggedy Andy asked in return.

''It was a rabbit!'' Fido cried. ''He ran right in here, for I could smell his tracks!''

''We could feel him!'' Raggedy Andy laughed.

''I could not tell you which way he went,'' Uncle Clem said, ''except I feel sure he came through the door and into the house!''

15

None of the dolls knew into which room the rabbit had run.

Finally, after much sniffing, Fido traced the rabbit to the nursery, where, when the dolls followed, they saw the rabbit crouching behind the rocking horse.

Fido whined and cried because he could not get to the rabbit and bite him.

"You should be ashamed of yourself, Fido!" cried Raggedy Ann. "Just see how the poor bunny is trembling!"

"He should not come scratching around our house if he doesn't care to be chased!" said Fido.

"Why don't you stay out in the woods and fields where you really belong?" Raggedy Andy asked the rabbit.

"I came to leave some Easter eggs!" the bunny answered in a queer little quavery voice.

"An Easter bunny!" all the dolls cried, jumping about and clapping their hands. "An Easter bunny!"

"Well!" was all Fido could say, as he sat down and began wagging his tail.

"You may come out from behind the rocking horse now, Easter bunny!" said Raggedy Andy. "Fido will not hurt you now that he knows, will you, Fido?"

"Indeed I won't!" Fido replied. "I'm sorry that I chased you! And I remember now, I had to jump over a basket out by the shed! Was that yours?"

"Yes, it was full of Easter eggs and colored grasses for the little girl who lives here!" the bunny said.

When the Easter bunny found out that Fido and the dolls were his friends, he came out from behind the rocking horse and hopped across the floor to the door.

"I must go see if any of the eggs are broken, for if they are, I will have to run home and color some more! I was just about to make a nice nest and put the eggs in it when Fido came bouncing out at me!"

And with a squeaky little laugh the Easter bunny, fol-

lowed by Fido and all the dolls, hopped across the lawn toward the shed. There they found the basket. Four of the lovely colored Easter eggs were broken.

"I will run home and color four more. It will only take a few minutes, so when I return and scratch again to make a nest, please do not bark at me!" said the Easter bunny.

"I won't! I promise!" Fido laughed.

"May we go with you and watch you color the Easter eggs?" Raggedy Andy begged.

"Indeed you may!" the Easter bunny answered. "Can you run fast?"

Then down through the garden and out through a crack in the fence the Easter bunny hopped, with a long string of dolls trailing behind.

When they came to the Easter bunny's home, they found Mama Easter bunny and a lot of little teeny-weeny bunnies who would someday grow up to be big Easter bunnies like their Mama and Daddy bunnies.

The Easter bunny told them of his adventure with Fido, and all joined in his laughter when they found it had turned out well in the end.

17

The Easter bunny put four eggs on to boil and while these were boiling he mixed up a lot of pretty colors.

When the eggs were boiled, he dipped them into the pretty colored dyes and then painted lovely flowers on them.

When the Easter bunny had finished painting the eggs he put them in his basket and, with all the dolls running along beside him, they returned to the house.

"Why not make the nest right in the nursery?" Raggedy Andy asked.

"That would be just the thing! Then the little girl would wonder and wonder how I could ever get into the

nursery without waking the rest of the folks, for she will never suspect that you dolls and Fido let me in!''

So with Raggedy Andy leading the way, they ran up to the nursery and there, way back in a corner, they watched the Easter bunny make a lovely nest and put the Easter eggs in it.

And in the morning, when Marcella came in to see the dolls, you can imagine her surprise when she found the pretty gift of the Easter bunny.

''How in the world did the bunny get inside the house and into this room without waking Fido?'' she laughed.

And Fido, pretending to be asleep, slowly opened one eye and winked over the edge of his basket at Raggedy Andy.

And Raggedy Andy smiled back at Fido, but never said a word.

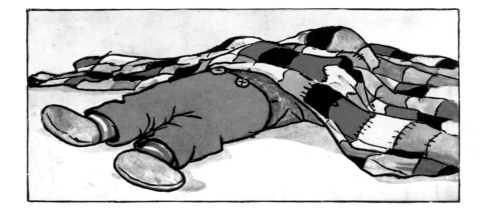

THE NEW TIN GUTTER

ALL DAY Saturday the men had worked up on the roof of the house and the dolls facing the window could see them.

The men made quite a lot of noise with their hammers, for they were putting new gutters around the eaves, and pounding upon tin makes a great deal of noise.

Marcella had not played with the dolls all that day, for she had gone visiting, so when the men hammered and made a lot of noise, the dolls could talk to each other without fear of anyone hearing or knowing they were really talking to each other.

"What are they doing now?" Raggedy Andy asked.

He was lying with his head beneath a little bed quilt, just as Marcella had dropped him when she left the nursery, so he could not see what was going on.

"We can only see the men's legs as they pass the window," answered Uncle Clem. "But they are putting new shingles or something on the roof!"

After the men had left their work and gone home to supper and the house was quiet, Raggedy Andy cautiously moved his head out from under the little bed quilt and, seeing that the coast was clear, sat up.

This was a signal for all the dolls to sit up and smooth out the wrinkles in their clothes.

21

The nursery window was open, so Raggedy Andy lifted the penny dolls to the sill and climbed up beside them.

Leaning out, he could look along the new shiny tin gutter the men had put in place.

''Here's a grand place to have a lovely slide!'' he said as he gave one of the penny dolls a scoot down the shiny tin gutter.

''*Whee!* See her go!'' Raggedy Andy cried.

All the other dolls climbed up on the windowsill beside him.

Scoot me, too!'' cried the other little penny doll in her squeaky little voice, and Raggedy Andy took her in his rag hand and gave her a great swing that sent her scooting down the shiny tin gutter, *''Kerswish!''*

Then Raggedy Andy climbed into the gutter himself and, taking a few steps, spread out his feet and went scooting down the shiny tin.

The other dolls followed his example and scooted along behind him.

When Raggedy Andy came to the place where he expected to find the penny dolls lying, they were nowhere about.

''Perhaps you scooted them farther than you thought!'' Uncle Clem said.

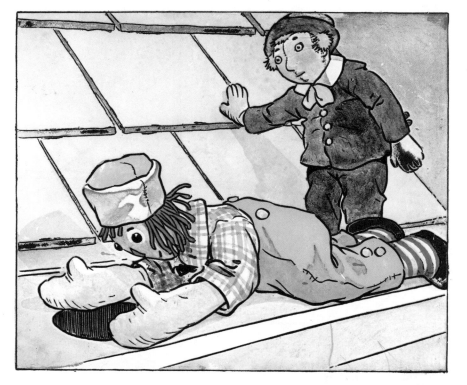

"Perhaps I did!" Raggedy Andy said. "We will look around the bend in the eave!"

"Oh dear!" he exclaimed when he had peeped around the corner of the roof. "The gutter ends here and there is nothing but a hole!"

"They must have scooted right into the hole," the Dutch doll said.

Raggedy Andy lay flat upon the shiny tin and looked down into the hole.

"Are you down there, penny dolls?" he called.

There was no answer.

"I hope their heads were not broken!" Raggedy Ann said.

"I'm so sorry I scooted them!" Raggedy Andy cried, as he brushed his hand over his shoe-button eyes.

"Maybe if you hold my feet, I can reach down the hole and find them and pull them up again!" he added.

Uncle Clem and the Dutch doll each took hold of one of Raggedy Andy's feet and let him slide down into the hole.

It was a rather tight fit, but Raggedy Andy wiggled and

twisted until all the dolls could see of him were his two feet.

"I can't find them!" he said in muffled tones. "Let me down farther and I think I'll be able to reach them!"

Now the Dutch doll and Uncle Clem thought that Raggedy Andy meant for them to let go of his feet and this they did.

Raggedy Andy kept wiggling and twisting until he came to a bend in the pipe and could go no farther.

"I can't find them!" he cried. "They have gone farther down the pipe! Now you can pull me up!"

"We can't reach you, Raggedy Andy!" Uncle Clem called down the pipe. "Try to wiggle back up a bit and we will catch your feet and pull you up!"

Raggedy Andy tried to wiggle backward up the pipe, but his clothes caught upon a little piece of tin that stuck out from the inside of the pipe and there he stayed. He could neither go down nor come back up.

"What shall we do?" Uncle Clem cried. "The folks will never find him down there, for we cannot tell them where he is, and they will never guess it!"

The dolls were all very sad. They stayed up on the shiny new tin gutter until it began raining and hoped and hoped that Raggedy Andy could get back up to them.

Then they went inside the nursery and sat looking out the window until it was time for the folks to get up and the house to stir. Then they went back to the position each had been in when Marcella had left them.

And although they were very quiet, each one was so sorry to lose Raggedy Andy, and each felt that he would never be found again.

"The rain must have soaked his cotton through and through!" sighed Raggedy Ann. "For all the water from the house runs down the shiny tin gutters and down the pipe into a rain barrel at the bottom!"

Then Raggedy Ann remembered that there was an opening at the bottom of the pipe.

"Tomorrow night, if we have a chance, we must take a stick and see if we can reach Raggedy Andy from the bottom of the pipe and pull him down to us!" she thought.

Marcella came up to the nursery and played all day, watching the rain patter upon the new tin gutter. She wondered where Raggedy Andy was, although she did not get worried about him until she had asked Mama where he might be.

"He must be just where you left him!" Mama said.

"I cannot remember where I left him!" Marcella said. "I thought he was with all the other dolls in the nursery, though!"

All day Sunday it rained and all of Sunday night, and Monday morning when Daddy started off to work it was still raining.

As Daddy walked out the front gate, he turned to wave good-bye to Mama and Marcella and then he saw something.

Daddy came right back into the house and called up the men who had put in the new shiny tin gutters.

"The drain pipe is plugged up. Some of you must have left shavings or something in the eaves, and it has washed down into the pipe, so that the water pours over the gutter in sheets!"

"We will send a man right up to fix it!" the men said.

So at about ten o'clock that morning one of the men came to fix the pipe.

But although he punched a long pole down the pipe, and punched and punched, he could not dislodge whatever it was that plugged the pipe and kept the water from running through it.

Then the man measured with his stick, so that he knew just where the place was, and with a pair of tin shears he cut

26

a section from the pipe and found Raggedy Andy.

Raggedy Andy was punched quite out of shape and all jammed together, but when the man straightened out the funny little figure, Raggedy Andy looked up at him with his customary happy smile.

The man laughed and carried little water-soaked Raggedy Andy into the house.

''I guess your little girl must have dropped this rag doll down into the drainpipe!'' the man said to Mama.

''I'm so glad you found him!'' Mama said to the man.

''We have hunted all over the house for him! Marcella could not remember where she put him, so when I get him nice and dry, I'll hide him in a nice easy place for her to find, and she will not know he has been out in the rain all night!''

So Mama put Raggedy Andy behind the radiator and there he sat all afternoon, steaming and drying out.

And as he sat there he smiled and smiled, even though there was no one to see him.

He felt very happy within and he always smiled, anyway, because his smile was painted on.

And another reason Raggedy Andy smiled was because he was not lonesome.

Inside his waist were the two little penny dolls.

The man had punched Raggedy Andy farther down into the pipe, and he had been able to reach the two little dolls and tuck them into a safe place.

"Won't they all be surprised to see us back again!" Raggedy Andy whispered as he patted the two little penny dolls with his soft rag hands.

And the two little penny dolls nestled against Raggedy Andy's soft cotton-stuffed body, and thought how nice it was to have such a happy, sunny friend.

DOCTOR RAGGEDY ANDY

RAGGEDY ANDY, Raggedy Ann, Uncle Clem and the Dutch doll were not given medicine because, you see, they had no mouths—that is, mouths through which medicine could be poured. Their mouths were either painted on, or were sewed on with yarn.

Sometimes the medicine spoon would be touched to their faces but none of the liquid would be given to them. Except accidentally.

But the French doll had a lovely mouth for taking medicine. It was open and showed her teeth in a dimpling smile. She also had soft brown eyes that opened and closed when she was tilted backward or forward.

The medicine that was given the dolls had great curing properties. It would cure the most stubborn case of croup, measles, whooping cough or any other ailment the dolls had wished upon them by their little mistress.

Some days all the dolls would be put to bed with measles, but in the course of half an hour they would have every other ailment in the doctor book.

The dolls enjoyed it very much, for, you see, Marcella always tried the medicine first to see if it was strong enough before she gave any to the dolls. So the dolls really did not get as much of the medicine as their little mistress.

The wonderful remedy was made from a very old recipe

31

handed down from ancient times. This recipe is guaranteed to cure every ill a doll may have. The medicine was made from brown sugar and water. Perhaps you may have used it for your dollies.

The medicine was also used as tea and soda water, except when the dolls were supposed to be ill.

Having nothing but painted or yarn mouths, the ailments of Raggedy Andy, Raggedy Ann, Uncle Clem and the Dutch doll mostly consisted of sprained wrists, arms and legs, or perhaps a headache and a toothache.

None of them knew they had the trouble until Marcella had wrapped up the injured rag arm, leg or head, and had explained in detail just what was the matter.

Raggedy Andy, Raggedy Ann, Uncle Clem or the Dutch doll were just as happy with their heads tied up for a toothache as they were without their heads tied up. Not having teeth, naturally they could not have a toothache, and if they could furnish amusement for Marcella by having her pretend they had a toothache, then that made them very happy.

So this day, the French doll was quite ill. She started out with the croup, and went through the measles, whooping cough and yellow fever in an hour.

The attack came on quite suddenly.

The French doll was sitting quietly in one of the little red chairs, smiling the prettiest of dimpling smiles at Raggedy Andy, and thinking of the romp the dolls would have that night after the house grew quiet when Marcella discovered that the French doll had the croup and put her to bed.

The French doll closed her eyes when put to bed, but the rest of her face did not change expression. She still wore her happy smile.

Marcella mixed very strong medicine and poured it into the French doll's open mouth.

She was given a dose every minute or so.

It was during the yellow fever stage that Marcella was called to supper and left the dolls in the nursery alone.

Marcella did not play with them again that evening, so the dolls all remained in the same positions until Marcella and the rest of the folks went to bed.

Then Raggedy Andy jumped from his chair and wound up the little music box. "Let's start with a lively dance!" he cried.

34

When the music started tinkling he caught the French doll's hand, and danced way across the nursery floor before he discovered that her soft brown eyes remained as closed as they were when she lay upon the sick bed.

All the dolls gathered around Raggedy Andy and the French doll.

"I can't open my eyes!" she said.

Raggedy Andy tried to open the French doll's eyes with his soft rag hands, but it was no use.

They shook her. This sometimes has the desired effect when dolls do not open their eyes.

They shook her again and again. It was no use! Her eyes remained closed.

"It must be the sticky, sugary medicine!" said Uncle Clem.

"I really believe it must be!" the French doll replied. "The medicine seemed to settle in the back of my head when I was lying down, and I can still feel it back there!"

"That must be it, and now it has hardened and keeps your pretty eyes from working!" said Raggedy Ann. "What shall we do?"

Raggedy Andy and Raggedy Ann walked over to a corner of the nursery and thought and thought. They pulled their foreheads down into wrinkles with their hands so that they might think harder.

Finally Raggedy Ann cried, "I've thought of a plan!" and went skipping from the corner out to where the other dolls sat around the French doll.

"We must stand her upon her head, then the medicine will run up into her hair, for there is a hole in the top of her head. I remember seeing it when her hair came off one time!"

"No sooner said than done!" cried Uncle Clem as he took the French doll by the waist and stood her upon her head.

"That should be long enough!" Raggedy Ann said,

when Uncle Clem had held the French doll in this position for about five minutes.

But when the French doll was again placed upon her feet her eyes still remained tightly closed.

All this time, Raggedy Andy had remained in the corner, thinking as hard as his rag head could think.

He thought and thought, until the yarn hair upon his head stood up in the air and wiggled.

"If the medicine did not run out into her hair when she stood upon her head," thought Raggedy Andy, "then it is because the medicine could not run, so, if the medicine cannot run, it is because it is too sticky and thick to run out the hole in the top of her head." He also thought a lot more.

At last he turned to the others and said out loud, "I can't seem to think of a single way to help her open her eyes unless we take off her hair and wash the medicine from inside her china head."

"Why didn't I think of that?" Raggedy Ann asked. "That is just what we shall have to do!"

So Raggedy Ann caught hold of the French doll's feet, and Raggedy Andy caught hold of the French doll's lively curls, and they pulled and they pulled.

Then the other dolls caught hold of Raggedy Ann and Raggedy Andy and pulled and pulled, until finally, with a sharp *"R-R-Rip!"* the French doll's hair came off, and the dolls who were pulling went tumbling over backward.

Laughingly they scrambled to their feet and sat the French doll up, so they might look into the hole in the top of her head.

Yes, the sticky medicine had grown hard and would not let the French doll's eyes open.

Raggedy Andy put his hand inside and pushed on the eyes so that they opened.

This was all right, only now the eyes would not close when the French doll lay down. She tried it.

So Raggedy Andy ran down into the kitchen and brought up a small tin cup full of warm water and a tiny rag.

With these he loosened the sticky medicine and washed the inside of the French doll's head nice and clean.

There were lots of cookie and cracker crumbs inside her head, too.

Raggedy Andy washed it all nice and clean, and then wet the glue, which made the pretty curls stay on.

So when her hair was placed upon her head again, the French doll was as good as new.

"Thank you all very much!" she said, as she tilted backward and forward, and found that her eyes worked very easily.

Raggedy Andy again wound up the little music box and, catching the French doll about the waist, started a rollicking dance that lasted until the roosters in the neighborhood began their morning crowing.

Then, knowing the folks might soon be stirring, the dolls left off their playing, and all took the same position they had been in when Marcella left them the night before.

And so Marcella found them.

The French doll was in bed with her eyes closed, and her happy dimpling smile lighting up her pretty face.

And to this day, the dollies' little mistress does not know that Raggedy Andy was the doctor who cured the French doll of her only illness.

MAKING "ANGELS" IN THE SNOW

"*WHEE!* It's good to be back home again!" said Raggedy Andy to the other dolls, as he stretched his feet out in front of the little toy stove and rubbed his rag hands briskly together, as if to warm them.

All the dolls laughed at Raggedy Andy for doing this, for they knew there had never been a fire in the little stove in all the time it had been in the nursery. And that was a long time.

"We are so glad and happy to have you back home again with us!" the dolls told Raggedy Andy. "For we have missed you very, very much!"

"Well," Raggedy Andy replied, as he held his rag hands over the tiny lid of the stove and rubbed them again, "I have missed all of you, too, and wished many times that you had been with me to join in and share in the pleasures and frolics I've had."

And as Raggedy Andy continued to hold his hands over the little stove, Uncle Clem asked him why he did it.

Raggedy Andy smiled and leaned back in his chair. "Really," he said, "I wasn't paying any attention to what I was doing! I've spent so much of my time while I was

41

away drying out my soft cotton stuffing it seems as though it has almost become a habit.''

''Were you wet most of the time, Raggedy Andy?'' the French doll asked.

''Nearly all the time!'' Raggedy Andy replied. ''First I would get sopping wet and then I'd freeze!''

''Freeze!'' exclaimed all the dolls in one breath.

''Dear me, yes!'' Raggedy Andy laughed. ''Just see here!'' And Raggedy Andy pulled his sleeve up and showed where his rag arm had been mended. ''That was quite a rip!'' he smiled.

''Dear! Dear! How in the world did it happen? On a nail?'' the Dutch doll asked as he put his arm about Raggedy Andy.

''Froze!'' said Raggedy Andy.

The dolls gathered around Raggedy Andy and examined the rip in his rag arm.

''It's all right now!'' he laughed. ''But you should have seen me when it happened! I was frozen into one solid cake of ice all the way through, and when Marcella tried to limber up my arm before it had thawed out, it went '*Pop!*' and just burst.

''Then I was placed in a pan of nice warm water until the icy cotton inside me had melted, and then I was hung up on a line above the kitchen stove, out at Grandma's.''

''But how did you happen to get so wet and then freeze?'' asked Raggedy Ann.

''Out across the road from Grandma's home, way out in the country, there is a lovely pond,'' Raggedy Andy explained. ''In the summertime pretty flowers grow about the edge, the little green frogs sit upon the pond lilies and beat upon their tiny drums all through the night and the twinkling stars wink at their reflections in the smooth water. But when Marcella and I went out to Grandma's, last week, Grandma met us with a sleigh, for the ground

was covered with starry snow. The pretty pond was covered with ice, too, and upon the ice was a soft blanket of the white, white snow. It was beautiful!'' said Raggedy Andy.

"Grandma had a lovely new sled for Marcella, a red one with shiny runners.

"And after we had visited Grandma a while, we went to the pond for a slide.

"It was heaps of fun, for there was a little hill at one end of the pond so that when we coasted down, we went scooting across the pond like an arrow.

"Marcella would turn the sled sideways, just for fun, and she and I would fall off and go sliding across the ice upon our backs, leaving a clean path of ice, where we pushed aside the snow as we slid. Then Marcella showed me how to make 'angels' in the soft snow!''

"Oh, tell us how, Raggedy Andy!'' shouted all the dollies.

"It's very easy!'' said Raggedy Andy. "Marcella would lie down upon her back in the snow and put her hands back up over her head, then she would bring her hands in a circle down to her sides, like this.'' And Rag-

gedy Andy lay upon the floor of the nursery and showed the dollies just how it was done. ''Then,'' he added, ''when she stood up it would leave the print of her body and legs in the white, white snow, and where she had swooped, her arms there were the 'angel's wings!' ''

''It must have looked just like an angel!'' said Uncle Clem.

''Indeed it was very pretty!'' Raggedy Andy answered. ''Then Marcella made a lot of 'angels' by placing me in the snow and working my arms. So you see, what with falling off the sled so much and making so many 'angels,' we both were wet, but I was completely soaked through. My cotton just became soppy and I was ever so much heavier! Then Grandma, just as we were having a most delightful time, came to the door and *'Oooh-hooed'* to Marcella to come and get a nice new doughnut. So Marcella, thinking to return in a minute, left me lying upon the sled and ran through the snow to Grandma's. And there I stayed and stayed until I began to feel stiff and could hear the cotton inside me go, *'Tic! Tic!'* as it began to freeze.

46

"I lay upon the sled until after the sun went down. Two little chickadees came and sat upon the sled and talked to me in their cute little bird language, and I watched the sky in the west get golden red, then turn into a deep crimson purple and finally a deep blue, as the sun went farther down around the bend of the earth. After it had been dark for some time, I heard someone coming through the snow and could see the yellow light of a lantern. It was Grandma.

"She pulled the sled over in back of her house and did not see that I was upon it until she turned to go in the kitchen. Then she picked me up and took me inside. 'He's frozen stiff as a board!' she told Marcella as she handed

47

me to her. Marcella did not say why she had forgotten to come for me, but I found out afterward that it was because she was so wet. Grandma made her change her clothes and shoes and stockings and would not permit her to go out and play again.

"Well, anyway," concluded Raggedy Andy, "Marcella tried to limber my arm and, being almost solid ice, it just burst. And that is the way it went all the time we were out at Grandma's. I was wet nearly all the time. But I wish you could all have been with me to share in the fun."

And Raggedy Andy again leaned over the little toy stove and rubbed his rag hands briskly together.

Uncle Clem went to the waste basket and came back with some scraps of yellow and red paper. Then, taking off one of the tiny lids, he stuffed the paper in part of the way as if the flames were shooting up!

Then, as all the dolls' merry laughter rang out, Raggedy Andy stopped rubbing his hands, and catching Raggedy Ann about the waist, he went skipping across the nursery floor with her, whirling so fast neither saw they had gone out through the door until it was too late. For coming to the head of the stairs, they both went head over heels, *"Blumpity, blump!"* over and over, until they wound up, laughing, at the bottom.

"Last one up is a rotten egg!" cried Raggedy Ann, as she scrambled to her feet. And with her skirts in her rag hands she went racing up the stairs to where the rest of the dollies stood laughing.

"Hurray, for Raggedy Ann!" cried Raggedy Andy generously. "She won!"

THE SINGING SHELL

FOR YEARS and years the beautiful shell had been upon the floor in Grandma's front room. It was a large shell with many points on it. These were coarse and rough, but the shell was most beautiful inside.

Marcella had seen the shell time and time again and often admired its lovely coloring, which could be seen when one looked inside the shell.

So one day, Grandma gave the beautiful shell to Marcella to have for her very own, up in the nursery.

"It will be nice to place before the nursery door so the wind will not blow the door closed and pinch anyone's fingers!" Grandma laughed.

So Marcella brought the shell home and placed it in front of the nursery door. Here the dolls saw it that night, when all the house was still, and stood about it wondering what kind of toy it might be.

"It seems to be nearly all mouth!" said the Dutch doll. "Perhaps it can talk."

"It has teeth!" the French doll pointed out. "It may bite!"

"I do not believe it will bite," Raggedy Andy mused, as he got down upon his hands and knees and looked up into the shell. "Marcella would not have it up here if it would bite!" And, saying this, Raggedy Andy put his rag arm into the lovely shell's mouth.

"It doesn't bite! I knew it wouldn't!" he cried. "Just feel how smooth it is inside!"

All the dolls felt and were surprised to find it polished so smoothly inside, while the outside was so coarse and rough. With the help of Uncle Clem and the Dutch doll, Raggedy Andy turned the shell upon its back, so that all the dolls might look in.

The coloring consisted of dainty pinks, creamy whites and pale blues, all running together just as the coloring in an opal runs from one shade into another. Raggedy Andy, stooping over to look farther up inside the pretty shell, heard something.

"It's whispering!" he said, as he raised up in surprise.

All the dolls took turns putting their ears to the mouth of the beautiful shell. Yes, truly it whispered, but they could not catch just what it said.

Finally Raggedy Andy suggested that all the dolls lie down upon the floor directly in front of the shell and keep very quiet.

"If we don't make a sound we may be able to hear what it says!" he explained.

So the dolls lay down, placing themselves flat upon the floor directly in front of the shell and where they could see and admire its beautiful coloring.

Now the dolls could be very, very quiet when they really wished to be, and it was easy for them to hear the faint whispering of the shell.

This is the story the shell told the dolls in the nursery that night:

"A long, long time ago, I lived upon the yellow sand, deep down beneath the blue, blue waters of the ocean. Pretty silken weeds grew up around my home and reached their waving branches up, up toward the top of the water.

"Through the pretty seaweed, fishes of pretty colors and shapes darted here and there, playing their games.

"It was still and quiet way down where I lived, for even if the ocean roared and pounded itself into an angry mass of tumbling waves up above, this never disturbed the calm waters down where I lived.

"Many times, little fishes or other tiny sea people came and hid within my pretty house when they were being pursued by larger sea creatures. And it always made me very happy to give them this protection.

"They would stay inside until I whispered that the larger creature had gone, then they would leave me and return to their play.

"Pretty little sea horses with slender, curving bodies often went sailing above me, or would come to rest upon my back. It was nice to lie and watch the tiny things curl their little tails about the seaweed and talk together, for the sea horses like one another and are gentle and kind to each other, sharing their food happily and smoothing their little ones with their cunning noses.

"But one day a diver leaped over the side of a boat and came swimming head first down, down to where I lay. My! How the tiny sea creatures scurried to hide from him. He took me in his hand and, giving his feet a thump upon the yellow sand, rose with me to the surface.

"He poured the water from me, and out came all the little creatures who had been hiding there!"

Raggedy Andy wiggled upon the floor, he was so interested.

"Did the tiny creatures get back into the water safely?" he asked the beautiful shell.

"Oh, yes!" the shell whispered in reply. "The man held me over the side of the boat, so the tiny creatures went safely back into the water!"

"I am so glad!" Raggedy Andy said, with a sigh of relief. "He must have been a kindly man!"

"Yes, indeed!" the beautiful shell replied. "So I was placed along with a lot of other shells in the bottom of the boat and every once in a while another shell was placed among us. We whispered together and wondered where we were going. We were finally sold to different people and I have been at Grandma's house for a long, long time."

"You lived there when Grandma was a little girl, didn't you?" Raggedy Ann asked.

"Yes," replied the shell, "I have lived there ever since Grandma was a little girl. She often used to play with me and listen to me sing."

"Raggedy Ann can play 'Peter, Peter, Pumpkin Eater' on the piano with one hand," said Uncle Clem, "but none of us can sing. Will you sing for us?" he asked the shell.

"I sing all the time," the shell replied, "for I cannot help singing, but my singing is a secret and so it is very soft

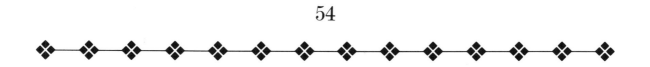

and low. Put your head close to the opening in my shell and listen!''

The dolls took turns doing this, and heard the shell sing softly and very sweetly.

''How strange and far away it sounds!'' exclaimed the French doll. ''Like Fairies singing in the distance! The shell must be singing the songs of the Mermaids and the Water Fairies!''

''It is strange that anything so rough on the outside could be so pretty within!'' said Raggedy Andy. ''It must be a great pleasure to be able to sing so sweetly!''

''Indeed it is,'' replied the beautiful shell, ''and I get great happiness from singing all the time.''

''And you will bring lots of pleasure to us, by being so happy!'' said Raggedy Andy. ''For although you may not enter into our games, we will always know that you are happily singing, and that will make us all happy!''

''I will tell you the secret of my singing,'' said the shell. ''When anyone puts an ear to me and listens, he or she hears the reflection of one's own heart's music, singing. So you see, while I say that I am singing all the time, in reality I sing only when someone full of happiness hears one's own singing as if it were mine.''

''How unselfish you are to say this!'' said Raggedy Andy. ''Now we are ever so much more glad to have you with us. Aren't we?'' he asked, turning to the rest of the dolls.

''Yes, indeed!'' came the answer from all the dolls, even the tiny penny dolls.

''That is why the shell is so beautiful inside!'' said Raggedy Ann. ''Those who are unselfish may wear rough clothes, but inside they are always beautiful, just like the shell, and reflect to others the happiness and sunny music within their hearts!''